The Reve of Captain Blood

PAUL SHIPTON

Illustrated by Judy Brown

Oxford University Press

OXFORD
UNIVERSITY PRESS

Oxford University Press, Great Clarendon Street, Oxford OX2 6DP

Oxford   New York
Athens Auckland Bangkok Bogotá Buenos Aires
Calcutta Cape Town Chennai Dar es Salaam Delhi
Florence Hong Kong Istanbul Karachi Kuala Lumpur
Madrid Melbourne Mexico City Mumbai Nairobi Paris
São Paulo Singapore Taipei Tokyo Toronto Warsaw

and associated companies in
Berlin Ibadan

Oxford is a trade mark of Oxford University Press

© Paul Shipton 1998
First published by Oxford University Press 1998
Reprinted 1998, 2000

ISBN 0 19 918580 8

Printed in Great Britain by Ebenezer Baylis

Illustrations by Judy Brown

Captain Blood

I thought I was going crazy when the
picture on the wall winked at me.

I must have walked past that portrait
of the pirate Captain Blood a million
times, but nothing like this had ever
happened before.

In the painting, a fearsome grin
beamed out from within the pirate's
bushy beard. A blue and red parrot sat
on his shoulder. The captain had a
gleam in his eyes – a look that hid
dreams of buried treasure and gold
doubloons.

Local legend said that Blood used to stay in our village, when he wasn't out at sea. He was the reason now why tourists came to our village – *and* why they came to stay at my mum and dad's Bed and Breakfast.

Usually, I didn't even give the picture a second glance, but today was different. A history professor from the university had been finding out about the story of Captain Blood. His name was Professor Grimsdale and he was staying at our B and B.

It was a big story round here and today, a TV crew was coming to hear what the professor had discovered.

I looked up at the picture of Captain Blood and spoke aloud.

Who CARES whether you were real or not? It all happened hundreds of years ago anyway...

And that's when the picture of Captain Blood winked at me.

I shook my head. Was I going mad?

The painting winked again. The
pirate's shark-like grin stretched even
wider.

And then the pirate just stepped out
from the painting.

I was too shocked to move a muscle.
The painting itself had not changed.
But now Captain Blood stood right
there in front of me as well. He was
still grinning.

I realized that I could see right through him. Could it be a...?

The pirate's wild eye fell on me.

What are ye staring at, boy? I've a good mind to feed ye to the sharks, ye scurvy dog.

Er... sorry?

The parrot on his shoulder gave a sigh.

He says 'hello'.

I glanced nervously at the door.
Could I get out? No, the see-through
pirate was blocking the way. 'Um, hello,'
I replied.

Well, what else could I say?

The pirate looked me up and down.

Not much to ye, eh, billy bones?
Ye'd make a good enough
cabin boy, I suppose.

He says he's
pleased to meet you.
His name is Captain Blood.
And I'm Hector. Nice to meet
you, I'm sure.

The pirate was gazing around. He pointed at the table and scratched his beard. 'What be this then?'

The parrot hissed, 'You mean – what IS this?'

The captain ignored him. He was looking at a model ship on the table. 'This is all wrong,' he said. 'The sails should be – HEY!'

He reached out for the ship but his hand went straight through it. It went through the table too.

What the...

Hector the parrot was calm.

Well, what did you expect? You ARE a ghost after all.

Now this was what I'd been thinking. But hearing the word said aloud – 'ghost' – made it all real for me.

So I fainted.

There's a job to do

I wasn't out for long. When I opened
my eyes, two faces were leaning
over me – two see-through
faces. I scrambled to
my feet.

That's better. We
can't be doing with
some lily-livered matey
who faints all the time.

That annoyed me a bit.

Hold on! What do
you think most
people would do
if they saw
a ghost?

11

The pirate shrugged.

Anyway, what are you doing here?

Blood's grin faded. But the parrot
seemed more sure of itself.

Well...I think we
ghosts only appear
when there's a job
to do. After all,
otherwise there'd
be ghosts everywhere,
wouldn't there?

This made sense.
The captain nodded too.

Then he looked puzzled. 'Aye, but what be the job?' he asked. Hector snapped, 'What IS the job? Well, I bet it has something to do with *them*.'

The bird jerked its beak towards the window. One of the TV crew was walking by.

Of course! The TV crew are here to hear Professor Grimsdale. He's been finding out all about YOU.

The pirate started towards the door.

I was thinking of the panic he would cause. But a hearty laugh escaped from the captain.

'Because I'm a ghost, lad? Don't worry yer head about that. You be the only one who can see or hear us.'

The parrot leaned forward.

We can only let one person see us. And we chose you.

The professor

It was true!

A small group had gathered in our front garden. We went and stood there and no one else saw the bulky pirate and his parrot.

After a few minutes Professor Grimsdale came out.

He glanced nervously at the people there. His eyes met mine for a moment, but they darted away quickly. I thought about how much the professor had changed since he first came to our Bed and Breakfast.

At first he had seemed nice, but then he'd grown less and less friendly.

The TV cameraman gave the signal to start.

> Ladies and gentlemen, as you know, I have been researching the so-called pirate known as Captain Blood.

The ghost by my side began to splutter.

> 'So-called pirate'? What do he mean?

> What DOES he mean?

> That be what I said.

17

I looked around. No one else could hear them arguing.

The professor smiled. 'After a lot of work, I am now sure that Captain Blood the pirate never existed.'

There were gasps of shock from the crowd. Professor Grimsdale held up a hand for silence. He went on, 'Oh, it's true there was a man who called himself "Captain Blood". But this was not his real name.

'My study of the historical papers and maps has shown that he was just a clever liar – a con man. He fooled everyone with his fantastic stories of life on the seven seas.'

The ghost of Captain Blood was
hopping around in rage. The parrot
had to hold on tight just to stay on his
shoulder.

A reporter lifted her hand.

What about the treasure?

All the stories said the pirate had
buried a chest full of treasure in the
area.

The professor shook his head.

I'm afraid there never was any buried treasure.

This was too much for the ghost of Captain Blood.

That bilge-rat! I'll make him walk the plank! I'll hang him from the yard-arm. Where's my cat o' nine tails? I'll —

I didn't understand it all, but I got the general idea – Captain Blood wasn't happy.

The parrot calmed him down at last.

The captain stopped. He looked like
a naughty child who has been told off.
The parrot turned to me.

X marks the spot

I was only allowed in guests' rooms in an 'emergency' (as my mum put it). But if this wasn't an emergency, what was?

'Quick!' I said. 'When Grimsdale has answered the reporters' questions, he'll come back to his room.'

Luckily it didn't take us long to find the papers. A small pile was sitting on a table in the corner and on the top lay an old map.

The captain swept it up in his meaty hand. I saw that it was a map of the coast near our village.

The captain jabbed a finger at the map.

'X marks the spot, lad. That's where the treasure is!'

A question leapt into my head.

Blood scratched his massive beard.

Aye, that's right, lad. What's going on?

Hector the parrot had an answer.

You can only touch things that belonged to you when you were alive. Like the map.

Just then we heard a noise – there were footsteps on the stairs, and they were coming this way.

CLUMP!
CLUMP!
CLUMP!

Pirate and parrot didn't move.

I looked around frantically for a hiding place. Under the bed!

I fell to the floor and slid myself under the bed. Then I waited.

The door opened. Footsteps clumped in the room. Then there was the sound of buttons being pushed on a telephone.

There was a pause as the person on the other end of the line spoke.

Grimsdale here.

Yes, yes, they believed everything. Now we can get the treasure without any problem.

A note of worry entered the professor's voice.

One thing — no one will get hurt, will they?

Then, after a moment, he sighed and said, 'OK. I'll bring the map and meet you right away.'

There was a rustle of papers, then the click of the door. Grimsdale had left.

When I stood up, Captain Blood was purple with rage. I thought he might blow up like a volcano.

He stopped and looked at the table. The map was gone.

'You must know where your own treasure is… Mustn't you?' I asked.

A puzzled expression came over the captain's face.

You CAN'T remember it?

'Well that was why I drew a map, lad. So I wouldn't HAVE to remember.'

'That's OK,' said the parrot, fluffing its feathers proudly. 'Now that we've seen it again, I can remember the whole map.'

Hector shows the way

Fifteen minutes later we were striding across the beach towards the spot marked on the map. I carried a shovel from our shed over my shoulder.

'Over 250 years,' agreed the parrot. But the captain was not worried.

At least there were no hotels or houses along here, I thought. Imagine if someone had built an amusement arcade right on top of the treasure!

As we walked, a question formed in my mind. I knew it wasn't polite, but I had to ask. After all, how often do you chat with a ghost?

Do you mind if I ask you something? How did you...you know...die?

'It was a big mistake, lad,' the captain said at last. 'I always thought I'd die at sea in battle. But it wasn't sword or cannon that got me. Not sharks either.'

He paused.

I said again, 'So how did you die?'
The parrot chipped in.

He choked on a chicken leg. I kept telling him not to gobble his food – but would he listen? Oh no, not the great Captain Blood.

The parrot gave the pirate a cross look.

What's worse, he fell right on top of me. Squashed me flat as a pancake. So I went as well.

The pirate looked thoughtful.

The trouble is, we were on land when we died. That means we're stuck here now. But all our mates are out at sea.

He sniffed the salty air and looked longingly in the direction of the sea.

We walked the rest of the way in silence. When we got closer Hector started telling us where to go.

Three paces east and...here. This is the spot!

We were on a piece of sandy waste land. The grey sea boomed in the distance.

The captain sat down.

OK, lad. Start diggin'!

I began to dig.

33

The sandy earth was soft, and at first the job wasn't too bad. But soon my shoulders began to ache. Then throb. My back felt as if an elephant had used it for a cushion.

Captain Blood tried to keep me going.

Not bad, matey. Keep goin'!

I wished he'd shut up.

I dug and dug. The hole grew deeper and deeper. My arms hurt more and more.

Nothing. Are you SURE this is the spot?

Parrot and pirate nodded.

I went on digging. Just when I was about to give up, my shovel struck something hard. Probably a gas pipe, I thought.

I dug some more until I could scrape the last layer of sand off the thing.

And there it was – the top of an old sea chest.

The captain hopped up and down in excitement.

There it be, lad. Me chest o' gold!

I even saw a flicker of interest in Hector's eyes. I dug deeper until we could see the catch. Then I noticed something else buried next to the chest.

Hey, what's this?

It was a sack, and inside there was a short, curved sword. It was rusty, but it looked usable.

'Me cutlass!' cried Captain Blood like someone greeting a long-lost friend.

Er...why did you bury your sword too?

'Ah well,' explained the pirate, 'I didn't want to show up at me poor old ma's with a sword, now did I? I thought I could pick it up later. How was I to know a chicken drumstick would do me in? I just –'

Hector the parrot cut in.

Ahem. I hate to interrupt, but some men are coming this way.

The battle on the beach

Three men were striding towards us and one was Professor Grimsdale! The two men with him both carried shovels. They didn't look as if they were after historical facts.

The captain watched with an eager glint in his eye. 'Stand your ground, lad,' he whispered. I was scared, but I did what I was told. I leaned against my shovel and waited.

When they reached us, one of the men gave me a frosty look.

Well, well. Looks like this kid has done our digging for us.

The men crowded round the hole. They peered down at the chest and I knew their brains were buzzing with the same thought – GOLD!

But the professor looked worried.

Now run along will you, Mark?

My heart was pounding.

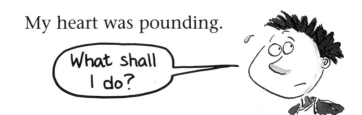

One of the other men growled, 'He said push off, kid.' He lifted the spade menacingly.

But I hadn't been speaking to them – I'd been speaking to the captain.

Blood didn't answer. The ghostly pirate bent down and took the cutlass in his hand.

Now let's see what you're made of, ye thieving bilge-rats!

Of course, Grimsdale and the two thugs could not see or hear the pirate. As far as they could tell, the cutlass simply floated up into the air. It waved at them menacingly.

The men looked terrified. I thought they were going to run, but then one of the thugs yelled.

It must be a trick! Just get the gold!

The thugs raised their spades and charged at the cutlass.

Captain Blood sprang into action. For such a big man he was startlingly quick.

He leapt between the two thugs with the grace of a ballet dancer.

Then he whacked one of them on
the backside with the flat of the sword.
He was laughing wildly.

The captain followed it up with a
rap on the top of the head.

The thug threw down his shovel and
fled. Captain Blood turned towards the
other thug.

Meanwhile the professor snatched the spade from my hands and jumped down into the hole. He was desperate to get at the chest.

I didn't try to stop the professor. I just watched as Captain Blood faced the second thug.

This one seemed tougher, but the captain made it look easy. The cutlass swept upwards and all the buttons flew off the man's shirt. His pale belly flopped out.

The man's eyes widened in fear and he pelted off too. I let out a cheer.

Just then, down in the hole, the
professor lifted the spade high above
his head. He brought it down on
the chest's rusty catch with a
sharp crack.

The catch snapped off.
Both Captain Blood and I froze at
the sound. This was it! We watched as
Grimsdale took hold of the lid and
slowly lifted it.

We all looked down into the chest and saw... nothing. It was empty. The smell of rotting wood filled my nose.

What? It can't be—

The professor looked stunned. He struggled to take a breath. His hands ran over the bottom of the chest as if something was hidden there.

But there was nothing.

If Grimsdale was shocked, I thought Captain Blood would be horrified.

But, no – the pirate was chuckling. His chuckles swelled into a full-blown laugh. He threw back his head and roared with laughter. Even the parrot smiled.

The captain saw my puzzled look.

'See those letters on the bottom of me chest?' he asked.

I bent down. The letters SB were carved into the wood.

The captain burst out laughing
again.

The professor scrambled out of the
hole. I'd almost forgotten about him.
He looked confused.

But before I could answer something caught my eye. Something out at sea. Something coming closer. I turned to watch it.

At first it was faint, but slowly it became clearer. It was a ship – a huge *ghostly* ship.

It seemed to float above the water. A black and white flag flew proudly from the main mast – the skull and crossbones!

A tear of joy trickled down Captain Blood's cheek into his beard.

It's me old ship! And all me mates!

A huge cheer went up from the pirates as they saw their captain. A pirate in a head scarf called out.

Cap'n, it's me - Seth. There's a chestful o'gold waitin' for ye on board!

The captain seemed lost for words.

Not Hector.

The captain tried to rest a hand on my shoulder. It went straight through.

And then the captain rose slowly
into the air until he reached the ship.

Captain Blood was back at last
with his crew of cut-throat pirates!
Then the ship turned and glided
away towards the open sea.

As it went, it grew fainter and fainter,
until at last I could see nothing.

But Captain Blood wasn't done yet. At the exact moment that it disappeared from my view, Professor Grimsdale let out a gasp. He was looking out to sea – to where the ghostly ship was.

Suddenly, I understood. Hector had said that they could choose just one person to see them. Before they left for ever, they had decided to let the professor see them. But why?

After a few minutes Grimsdale
turned to me. His eyes were watery
with tears.

The professor looked back out to sea.

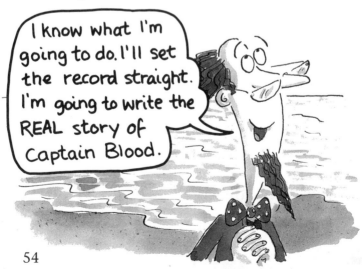

He paused for a moment and I could see his brain was working overtime.

There was a whirlpool of thoughts in my head – thoughts like 'The past isn't really dead,' and 'History is more than just dusty old books.' It was hard to put them into words. All I said was this.

About the author

When I was growing up
in Manchester, I always
wanted to be an
astronaut, a footballer,
or (if those didn't work
out for any reason)
perhaps a rock star.
So it came as something
of a shock when I

became first a teacher and then an
editor of educational books.

I have lived in Cambridge, Aylesbury,
Oxford and Istanbul. I'm still on the run and
now live in Chicago with my wife and family.

On family holidays by the sea, I often
looked for buried treasure. Did I find any?
What do you think?

Other Treetops books at this level include:
The Monster in the Wardrobe by Paul Shipton
Black Dan by Susan Gates
The Goalie From Nowhere by Alan MacDonald
Bones! by Paul Shipton
Spooky! by Michaela Morgan

Also available in packs
Stage 13 pack C   0 19 918585 9
Stage 13 class pack C   0 19 918586 7